FIONA WATERS is a well-known figure in the children's book world.
For many years she managed Heffer's Children's Bookshop in Cambridge.
She was also a consultant on Yorkshire Television's award-winning series
"The Book Tower". She is the editor of many prestigious anthologies including
The Cat King's Daughter (Methuen), *The Bloomsbury Book of Christmas Poetry*,
Footprints on the Page and *Dark as a Midnight Dream* (both Evans).
Golden Apples (Heinemann, 1985) and *The Poetry Book* (Orion, 1996)
were both shortlisted for the Signal Poetry Award.
Her first collection of her own poems, *Eyewitness Funfax*, was published in 1997
(Henderson), and her retelling of an Arabian Nights story,
The Brave Sister (Bloomsbury Classics) came out in 1998.

SOPHY WILLIAMS took a degree in graphic art at Kingston Polytechnic
and in 1988 was runner-up in the Reader's Digest Young Illustrators Competition.
In 1981 her first illustrated book, *When Grandma Came*, written by
Jill Paton Walsh (Viking/Puffin), was runner-up for the Mother Goose Award.
Among Sophy's many other books are Michael Rosen's *Moving*,
Peter Elbling's *Aria* (both Viking),
Robert Nye's *Lord Fox and Other Spine-Chilling Tales* and Adrian Mitchell's
My Cat Mrs Christmas (both Orion). *The Orchard Book of Starry Tales*,
written by Geraldine McCaughrean, is her latest publication.

CAT
IN THE
DARK
A FLURRY OF FELINE VERSE

Chosen by Fiona Waters
Illustrated by Sophy Williams

FRANCES LINCOLN

*For Betty Firth with much love,
and special memories of Plush* ~F.W.

To my mother and father ~S.W.

• CONTENTS •

TICK‑A‑LICK 6

AUNTIE AGNES'S CAT...... 8

ORANGE PAW MARKS..... 10

WATERCAT 12

MY UNCLE PAUL
OF PIMLICO 14

CATS.................... 16

CATAPILLOW............. 18

FOOTPRINTS IN
THE SNOW................ 21

OLD TOM 23

AS I WAS GOING TO
ST IVES................. 25

CAT IN THE DARK........ 26

CAT WARMTH............28

TICK-A-LICK

Tick-a-lick cat time,
Paw lick, ear lick, whiskers.
Tick-a-lick tail flick,
Fur time, feather time,
Leaves scuffle, time shuttle,
Mouse house, cheese fleas,
Scratch thatch,
Open fire, cowbyre.

Tick-a-lick lap time,
Saucer lick, bowl lick, whiskers.
White, milk, drops.
Tick-a-lick sleep time,
Stretch out, claws out,
Fire's out.

Tick-a-night crouch time,
Pounce it, crunched it, whiskers.
Tick-a-lick witches,
Broom-stick, moon-tricks,
Trouble bubble, prickly stubble,
Screech, retch,
Hallowe'en
Midnight.

Tick-a-lick moon's out,
Stars out, fire's out.
Tick-a-day night's out.
Tick-a-lick a
Tick-a-lick-
a tick-
a

Rona M. Campbell

6

AUNTIE AGNES'S CAT

My Auntie Agnes has a cat.
I do not like to tell her that
Its body seems a little large
(With lots of stripes for camouflage).
Its teeth and claws are also larger
Than they ought to be. A rajah
Gave her the kitten, I recall,
When she was stationed in Bengal.
But that was many years ago,
And kittens are inclined to grow.
So now she has a fearsome cat —
But I don't like to tell her that.

Colin West

ORANGE PAW MARKS

Orange paw marks from the paint tin,
Orange paw marks in the yard,
Orange paw marks in the kitchen
And past the fire-guard.

Orange paw marks on the table,
Orange paw marks on the floor,
Orange paw marks on the high chair,
Orange paw marks to the door.

Orange paw marks up the staircase,
It's an orange patterned path,
Orange paw marks on the landing,
Orange paw marks in the bath.

Orange paw marks in our bedroom,
On the patchwork eiderdown,
Orange paw marks in the cot
And on my sister's dressing-gown.

Orange paw marks on the carpets,
'Orange paw marks!' my Dad wails
As he follows all the winding,
Crossing orange paw mark trails.

When you leave the lid off paint
And you have a nosy cat,
The result is orange paw marks,
Oh, please remember that!

Michelle Magorian

10

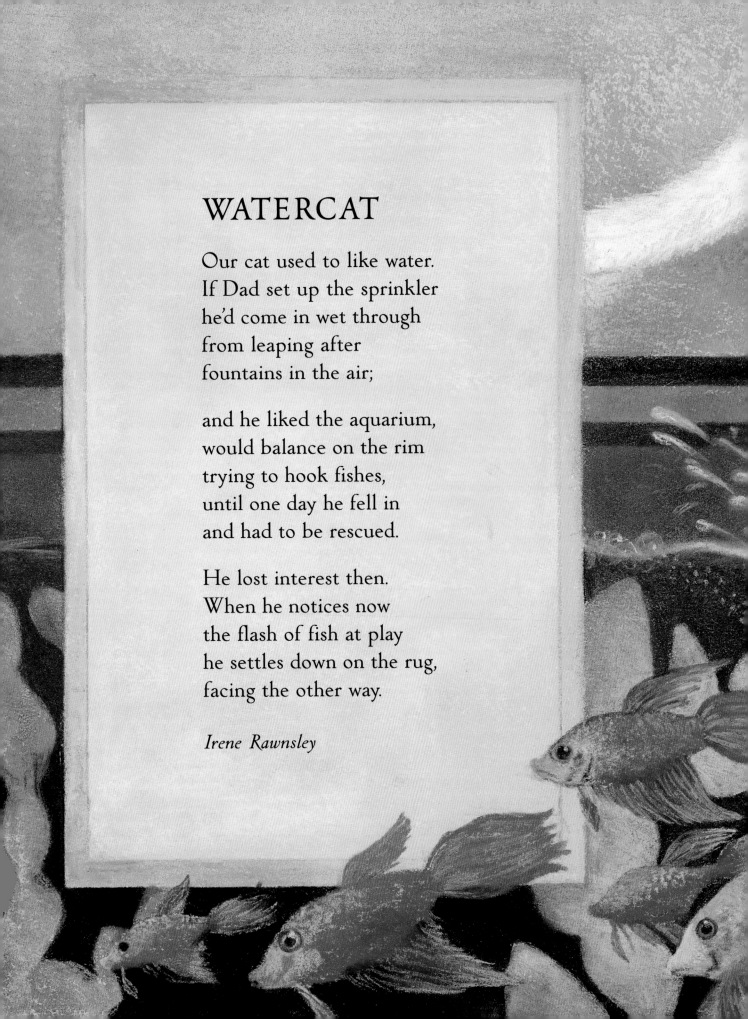

WATERCAT

Our cat used to like water.
If Dad set up the sprinkler
he'd come in wet through
from leaping after
fountains in the air;

and he liked the aquarium,
would balance on the rim
trying to hook fishes,
until one day he fell in
and had to be rescued.

He lost interest then.
When he notices now
the flash of fish at play
he settles down on the rug,
facing the other way.

Irene Rawnsley

MY UNCLE PAUL
OF PIMLICO

My Uncle Paul of Pimlico
Has seven cats as white as snow,
Who sit at his enormous feet
And watch him, as a special treat,
Play the piano upside-down,
In his delightful dressing gown;
The firelight leaps, the parlour glows,
And, while the music ebbs and flows,
They smile (while purring the refrains),
At little thoughts that cross their brains.

Mervyn Peake

CATS

It's said that cats have magic powers
Because they talk to stones and flowers
And stalk the ghosts and midnight elves
That dwell among the kitchen shelves
Despite the rumours of black magic
The truth, alas, is frankly tragic
For though they look extremely wise
It should not fill you with surprise
To learn that cats are rather dense
Possessing little common sense
Since cats have brains the size of peas
They're scarcely smarter than their fleas

Miles Gibson

CATAPILLOW

A catapillow
is a useful pet

To keep
upon your bed

Each night you simply
fluff him up

Then rest
your weary head.

Roger McGough

FOOTPRINTS IN THE SNOW

When the cats make tracks,
there's just one set of tracks . . .

When they jump from the window
they put their feet in the same places.

This proves, as you ought to know,
that cats don't like snow.

Gavin Ewart

OLD TOM

Old Tom is tabby
With some grey on his nose.
Old Tom is shabby
And wears old clothes.

Old Tom is crabby –
He growls and he bites.
Old Tom is scabby,
With scars of old fights.

His tongue's like a grater
His ears are both ragged.
His tail's like a taper
And his teeth are all jagged.

Most of the day
He takes forty winks.
If you ask him to play
He just growls, yawns, and blinks.

Geoffrey Summerfield

AS I WAS GOING
TO ST IVES

As I was going to St Ives
I met a man with seven wives;
Every wife had seven sacks;
Every sack had seven cats;
Every cat had seven kits.
Kits, cats, sacks, and wives –
How many were going to St Ives?

Anon

CAT IN THE DARK

Mother, Mother, what was that?
Hush, my darling! Only the cat.
(Fighty-bitey, ever-so-mighty)
Out in the moony dark.

Mother, Mother, what was that?
Hush, my darling! Only the cat.
(Prowly-yowly, sleepy-creepy,
Fighty-bitey, ever-so-mighty)
Out in the moony dark.

Mother, Mother, what was that?
Hush, my darling! Only the cat.
(Sneaky-peeky, cosy-dozy,
Prowly-yowly, sleepy-creepy,
Fighty-bitey, ever-so-mighty)
Out in the moony dark.

Mother, Mother, what was that?
Hush, my darling! Only the cat.
(Patchy-scratchy, furry-purry,
Sneaky-peeky, cosy-dozy,
Prowly-yowly, sleepy-creepy,
Fighty-bitey, ever-so-mighty)
Out in the moony dark.

Margaret Mahy

CAT WARMTH

All afternoon,
My cat sleeps,
On the end of my bed.

When I creep my toes
Down between the cold sheets,
I find a patch of cat-warmth
That he's left behind;
An invisible gift.

John Cunliffe

Cat in the Dark copyright © Frances Lincoln Limited 1999
Selection copyright © Fiona Waters 1999
Illustrations copyright © Sophy Williams 1999

First published in Great Britain in 1999 by
Frances Lincoln Limited, 4 Torriano Mews
Torriano Avenue, London NW5 2RZ

The Publishers gratefully acknowledge permission to reproduce the following:
"Tick-a-lick", by permission of Rona Campbell; "Auntie Agnes's Cat", by permission
of Colin West; "Orange Paw Marks", by permission of Viking; "Watercat",
by permission of Methuen Children's Books; "My Uncle Paul of Pimlico", from
A Pot of Gold (Doubleday, 1989), by permission of David Higham Associates; "Cats",
copyright © 1994 Miles Gibson, reprinted by kind permission of Jonathan Clowes Ltd.,
London, on behalf of Miles Gibson; "Catapillow", reprinted by permission of
The Peters Fraser and Dunlop Group Limited on behalf of Roger McGough, copyright
© Roger McGough, 1988; "Footprints in the Snow", by permission of Margo Ewart;
"Old Tom", text © Geoffrey Summerfield, 1983, first published by Andre Deutsch
Children's Books, an imprint of Scholastic Ltd.; "Cat in the Dark", by permission of
Vanessa Hamilton Books Ltd.; "Cat Warmth", by permission of David Higham Associates.

First paperback edition 2000

British Library Cataloguing in Publication Data
available on request

ISBN hardback 0-7112-1353-4
ISBN paperback 0-7112-1476-X

Set in Pastonchi and Baker Signet

Printed in Hong Kong
1 3 5 7 9 8 6 4 2